THE VOYAGE OF
THE PURPLE PRAWN

BUNCH OF
BADDIES

THE CACTUS BOYS

**CAPTAIN MIDNIGHT AND
THE GRANNY BAG**

GALACTACUS THE AWESOME

**THE VOYAGE OF
THE PURPLE PRAWN**

THE VOYAGE OF
THE PURPLE PRAWN

Andrew Matthews

Illustrated by
André Amstutz

ORCHARD BOOKS

for Marc
A.M.

CB
/5f/c

070b973099

ORCHARD BOOKS
96 Leonard Street, London EC2A 4RH
Orchard Books Australia
14 Mars Road, Lane Cove, NSW 2066
ISBN 1 85213 781 9 Hardback
ISBN 1 85213 878 5 Paperback
First published in Great Britain 1995
Text © Andrew Matthews 1995
Illustrations © André Amstutz 1995
The right of Andrew Matthews to be identified as the Author
and André Amstutz as the Illustrator of this Work
has been asserted by them in accordance with
the Copyright, Designs and Patents Act, 1988.
A CIP catalogue record for this book is available
from the British Library.
Printed in Great Britain.

CONTENTS

1

THE GULPING PELICAN

IT was a rowdy night at The Gulping Pelican. Pirates from all over the Spanish Main jostled together in the taproom of the inn. They drank grog, sang songs and did dangerous things with cutlasses and pistols.

Of all the bold buccaneers gathered at

The Gulping Pelican, the boldest and
bristliest was Abel Thinscratch. He was a
big man, with a round stomach and a
beard that was bristlier than a hedgehog's
behind. On his left shoulder perched
Lucan, his pet toucan. Lucan wore a patch
over one eye, had a long, sharp beak and
knew such rude words that when he
swore, the air went stiffer than a tray of
meringues.

Abel Thinscratch was captain of *The Purple Prawn,* and his crew were the scum of the Seven Seas. When law-abiding sea captains saw *The Purple Prawn* approaching, they went as white as an albatross's underneath, and their rich passengers locked themselves in their cabins and jibbered like frightened baboons.

Yet, despite his awesome reputation, Captain Thinscratch was not content. As he sat sipping grog with some members of his crew, a deep frown creased his eyebrows.

"What's up, captain?" asked Benbow Dobbs, the first mate, as he wiped his lips with the back of his hairy hand. "Your face looks longer than a conger eel."

"Tornado Truman, that's what's up!" rumbled Captain Thinscratch. "'E's got a more rascally reputation than mine, and I can't stand it! Every time I do somethin', 'e goes one better. I won't rest until I'm a bigger rogue than 'e is."

"Tell you what, skipper," said Mussels Muldoon, the ship's cook, tapping the side of his long, thin nose. "They say a Dutch

11

galleon loaded with silver is settin' sail from Cuba in two days' time and – "

"Not another Dutch galleon!" groaned Captain Thinscratch. "I'm fed up to the scuppers with 'em!"

Dab Hands, the master-gunner, put down his mug of grog and dug Captain Thinscratch in the ribs with a bony elbow. "'Ow about a little cruise out to Bermuda?" he suggested. "We could rob a rich plantation or two."

"Kids' stuff!" scoffed Captain Thinscratch. "I want to do somethin' different! Somethin' original! Somethin' that'll make Tornado Truman turn turquoise with envy."

"Perhaps I can be of assistance," said a voice.

The voice sounded like a vole choking on a pond-snail and it belonged to a stranger who was huddled over the next table. The stranger was a short, scrawny man, wrapped up so tightly in a long, black cloak that at first glance the pirates mistook him for a lumpy shadow.

"Allow me to introduce myself," said the stranger. "My name is Crispin Chickweed. I've travelled here all the way from England to talk to you about Captain Blubber's treasure chart."

The pirates were astonished at his words. Captain Thinscratch's hand flew to his neck and his fingers closed over something hidden inside his shirt. "What d'you know about Captain Blubber's chart?" he gasped.

"I'm a debt-collector by trade," said Crispin Chickweed. "Last year I happened to call on an old pirate living in a hovel near Harwich. He had no money to pay his debts, but he gave me half of Captain Blubber's map and he told me that you had the other half."

"I've never heard such a bucket of bilge in all my life!" snorted Captain Thin-scratch. "What was the name of this old pirate?"

"Walrus-Breath Watkin," came the reply. Captain Thinscratch's eyes went as round as cannon-balls, Benbow's pigtail unravelled itself, Mussels' thin nose went pink and twitched and Dab's eyebrows lifted up so high that they disappeared under the edge of the red handkerchief that was tied round his head. Lucan the Toucan flapped his wings and squawked.

Singe me sea-boots!

"Walrus-Breath Watkin was Captain Blubber's bosun!" Captain Thinscratch whispered to himself. Then he calmed down and a sly look came into his eyes. "I've got my 'alf of the chart 'ere in me shirt," he said to Crispin Chickweed. "What say we put both 'alves together on the table right this minute, matey?"

The pirates exchanged knowing glances and low chuckles at this.

"Impossible," said Crispin Chickweed pointing to his head. "You see, my half of the chart is up here."

"What, in your 'ood?" cried Benbow.

"No, in my memory," explained Crispin Chickweed. "If you want to find Captain Blubber's treasure, gentlemen, you're going to have to take me with you."

2

THE CAPTAIN'S TABLE

NEXT morning, bright and early, a secret meeting was held in the captain's cabin on board *The Purple Prawn*. Crispin Chickweed, Benbow Dobbs, Mussels Muldoon and Dab Hands watched closely as Captain Thinscratch reached inside his shirt and drew out a piece of tatty parchment, which he spread on the table. The writing on the parchment was so thin and wriggly that it looked as if a spider had fallen into an ink-pot and crawled across the page. The writing said:

If you would have my treasure
Then you must sail to
And if my treasure
First proceed

Go south-east,
Through the
Then take the path
To the rock where
From there, southwards
Through jungle thick
If you
Then at
There is
Wherein

BEAKY
CREEK

MANGROVE
SWAMP

"That's my 'alf of old Blubber's treasure chart," declared Captain Thinscratch. "I won it by cheatin' in a pirates' spittin' contest." He turned to Crispin Chickweed and fixed him with a stare sharp enough to prise a winkle out of its shell. "And now it's time for you to tell us what the missin' part says, shipmate," he said.

"Aha!" Crispin Chickweed said knowingly. "If I tell you everything, what's to stop you throwing me overboard and taking the treasure for yourself? How do I know I can trust you?"

"Of course you can't trust me!" hooted Captain Thinscratch. "I'm a notorious pirate and I've got my reputation to think of! I'm famous for bein' the sneakiest, slyest and lowest-down swab 'oo ever sailed – except for Tornado Truman, of course, drat 'im!"

"In that case," said Crispin Chickweed, "I'm only going to tell you a bit at a time."

"Mouldy mizzen-masts!" cursed Captain Thinscratch. "That's scuppered all my schemes of skulduggery!"

Crispin Chickweed raised his hand to his mouth and cleared his throat. "The beginning goes like this," he said.

If you would have my treasure . . . **pile**
Then you must sail to . . . **Parrot Isle.**

PARROTS? Blast their barnacles!

"Stow that screechin', you feathered fool!" growled Captain Thinscratch.

23

"Benbow, hoist all the sails and set a course south-south-east!"

"Aye-aye, skipper!" said Benbow.

"Dab!" barked Captain Thinscratch. "Get down on the gun-deck and load up the cannon! If Tornado Truman gets wind of this and tries to stop us, we'll blast 'im clean out of the water."

"Right you are, cap'n!" grinned Dab.

"Mussels!" snapped Captain Thinscratch. "Scuttle off to the galley and cook us up a sizzlin', 'earty, pirate-style breakfast!"

"At once, sir!" said Mussels.

"Er, if it wouldn't be too much bother, I'd rather have a piece of dry toast and a cup of weak tea," said Crispin Chickweed.

"Tea and toast?" Captain Thinscratch repeated scornfully. "That kind of pap's only fit for lily-livered landlubbers! When you go sailin' with a crew of rollickin' rascals like us, you need some decent grub inside you! A big plate of fried eggs and sausages, with a ship's biscuit to mop up the grease and a foamin' tankard of strong ale to wash it all down – that's the stuff!"

Crispin Chickweed's face went the colour of cold porridge. "Um, oh dear!" he said. "I'm afraid that when I'm on a boat, the rocking makes me come over all collywobbly."

"Never mind, matey!" laughed Captain Thinscratch. "When we're out on the open ocean, you'll soon find your sea-legs."

"My legs are fine," said Crispin Chickweed. "It's my sea-stomach that worries me."

"Rest easy, mess-mate," said Captain Thinscratch. "I've got a feelin' at the back of my neck that tells me this voyage is goin' to be as smooth as a swan swimmin' across a mill-pond."

And, strangely enough, the back of Captain Thinscratch's neck was completely wrong. *The Purple Prawn* sailed smack into the middle of a tropical storm that hammered the deck with huge waves, ripped the sails and blew the ship off course.

When the storm finished, there was no wind at all and *The Purple Prawn* floated motionless for two days of blistering heat. When the weather finally cooled and a breeze began to blow, the pirates sailed across the path of a British man-of-war. The man-of-war gave chase and they only managed to escape when night fell.

All this time, Crispin Chickweed lay groaning in a hammock in the captain's cabin.

"Devil take that debt-collector!" Benbow Dobbs told Captain Thinscratch. "He's brought a curse on to this ship!"

"I'll 'ave no talk of curses 'ere!" Captain Thinscratch said sternly. "Bad luck comes in threes. First there was the storm, then we were becalmed, then we met the man-of-war. That makes three and that means all our bad luck's been used up for this – "

He had been going to say "voyage", but at that moment *The Purple Prawn* sailed through a gap in the reef around Parrot Isle and stuck fast.

3

MANGROVES AND DODOS

AT first light, Captain Thinscratch, Benbow, Mussels and Dab hauled a groaning Crispin Chickweed out of his hammock. The debt-collector was wobblier than a loose tooth.

Captain Thinscratch held up the torn chart. "Well," he said, "'ere we are at

Parrot Isle ... almost. Where now, matey?"

Crispin Chickweed took a deep, shuddery breath and croaked.

And if my treasure... you would seek,
First proceed... to Beaky Creek,
Go south-east... and take a stomp
Through the... manky mangrove swamp.

A longboat was lowered over the side of
The Purple Prawn. Captain Thinscratch
and his men helped Crispin Chickweed
aboard and rowed towards the island. It
took an hour to find Beaky Creek and the
mangrove swamp. Benbow tied the
longboat to a mossy branch, and then they
all set off stomping south-east.

The swamp was a terrible place. Soft, evil-smelling mud sucked at their boots, tangled mangrove roots tripped them up, fiddler crabs nipped them and flying insects used them as a restaurant.

"No point in rushin', men," advised

Captain Thinscratch. "Let's save our strength."

Crispin Chickweed was feeling a little better now that he was on land, even if it was soggy, but something was worrying him. He tugged at Captain Thinscratch's sleeve. "I don't like to make a fuss, captain," he said, "but a tree trunk has been following us for the last five minutes."

Captain Thinscratch looked behind and saw a long, knotty log floating in muddy swamp-water. "You must 'ave a touch of sea-fever, matey," the captain said. "That's nothin' but an old lump of wood. It can't possibly be followin' us!"

Just then, the log opened a pair of yellow eyes and smiled a wide alligator smile.

"Ah!" said Captain Thinscratch. "In that case, men, I reckon as 'ow it might be wiser for us to run for our lives!"

The pirates and Crispin Chickweed stumbled and squelched through the swamp as fast as they could. At last, they reached dry ground and came to a stony path that twisted away through a grove of coconut palms.

"That must be the way," panted Crispin Chickweed.

"But the last dodo died off years ago!" said Benbow, flicking a crab off the top of one of his boots.

"Old Blubber must've gone clean off 'is crows' nest," quipped Dab.

Laughing heartily, the little band followed the path through the palms. They had only gone a few paces, when they heard a cry that stopped their laughter and chilled their spines.

"What was that?" quailed Crispin Chickweed.

Captain Thinscratch narrowed his eyes and drew a pistol from his belt. "When I was out in the East Indies, I 'eard the roar of an 'ungry, man-eatin' tiger," he said. "I only 'eard it once, but it's not a noise you can forget in an 'urry. I tell you now that what we just 'eard was nothin' like it, but we'd better go quietly and keep our eyes peeled."

"It sounded more like a donkey than a man-eating tiger," said Crispin Chickweed.

"Maybe it was a man-eatin' donkey," Benbow said grimly. "You get some strange creatures round these parts."

They pressed on, keeping close together and flinching whenever a twig snapped underfoot. The strange cry came again, sounding closer, and more cries answered it.

"Must be a pack of 'em!" Mussels hissed.

"And we're 'eadin' straight for 'em!" said Dab.

"I wonder what they can be?" mused Crispin Chickweed. "Oooh, I love surprises!"

"Belay that yabberin'!" rasped Captain Thinscratch. "There's somethin' up a'ead!"

Five pairs of eyes peered nervously through the palms and saw a black rock sticking up out of the ground. Big, grey birds waddled over the rock. The birds had stubby wings and sharp-looking beaks, and as they waddled they called to each other in voices that sounded like a herd of donkeys having an argument. "Why, they're dodos!" exclaimed Captain Thinscratch.

"Ugly, ain't they?" said Benbow.

"Those beaks look as though they could do you a nasty," said Crispin Chickweed.

"Stuff and nonsense!" Captain Thinscratch guffawed. "'Tis a well-known fact that dodos are friendly birds and gentle as lambs!"

But the dodos of Parrot Isle didn't seem to know anything about this. As soon as

they caught sight of the intruders, they charged at them, furiously snapping their beaks.

"If I may be so bold as to make a suggestion, captain, I think we should hop it sharpish!" said Crispin Chickweed.

"I'm inclined to your way of thinkin'," said the captain. "Which direction?"

"South," said Crispin Chickweed, "according to the chart."

From there, southwards . . .
            lies your way
Through jungle thick . . .
        where mambas play.

With angry dodos pecking at their legs, the men ran.

4

CAPTAIN BLUBBER'S
TREASURE CHEST

THE dodos stopped their chase at the edge of the jungle, and it wasn't long before Captain Thinscratch and the others found out why. There was no path, so they had to hack their way through with cutlasses. Even Crispin Chickweed had to lend a hand and he slashed at the

undergrowth with his penknife. Every step of the way the men were hissed at by venomous mambas and pelted with rotten mangoes by howler-monkeys, who hooted at them from the tree-tops. Branches lashed their faces and thorny vines ripped their clothes.

"Hmm!" said Crispin Chickweed. "This reminds me that I must weed my back garden when I get home."

Captain Thinscratch turned to him, wild-eyed. "Home?" he cried. "We're never goin' to get 'ome, d'you 'ear? This jungle is a green 'ell and we're doomed to wander in it for ever!"

"Chin up, captain," said Crispin Chickweed. "I know we've been nipped by crabs, bitten by insects and pecked by extinct birds, but it can't be much further, according to the chart."

If you ... manage to survive
Then at ... Perch Hill you will arrive.
There is ... a cave on the south side
Wherein ... my treasure I did hide.

"Think of the treasure, skipper!" urged Benbow.

"Aye!" said Mussels. "Think of the diamonds and rubies!"

"Think of doubloons runnin' through your fingers in a golden shower!" whispered Dab.

"Or think of a nice hot bath and a mug of cocoa," said Crispin Chickweed.

"You're right!" Captain Thinscratch croaked hoarsely. "I'll think about Tornado Truman's face when 'e 'ears about this darin' exploit. Why, 'e'll be so peeved, 'e'll paint 'is poop-deck pink!"

Somehow, the men found the strength to struggle on until they eventually emerged from the jungle.

"I can't go no further!" groaned Captain Thinscratch, collapsing on to the ground.

"Nor can I!" wailed Benbow, tumbling behind him.

Too tired to complain, Mussels and Dab fell onto their backs and wheezed like punctured footballs. Only Crispin Chickweed stayed on his feet and he pointed with a trembling, mango-stained finger.

"Look there!" he exclaimed. "That must be Perch Hill! We've made it!"

The pirates raised their weary heads and saw a hill before them. It was shaped rather like a parrot sitting on a perch.

"That's it!" said Captain Thinscratch. "I'm just a few steps away from fame and fortune!"

The sight of Perch Hill gave Crispin Chickweed and the pirates new strength. So eager were they to find the treasure that

they almost ran. The cave was easy to find. With trembling fingers, Captain Thinscratch lit a stub of candle with the aid of a tinder-box and held it up to the shadows in the cave mouth. "Forward, men!" he whispered excitedly.

The men formed a line behind the captain and they entered the cave. The candle light reflected back off slimy walls and the air smelled terrible.

"What's that putrid pong?" Crispin
Chickweed asked with a cough.

"Bats' droppin's, shipmate," Mussels
informed him. "The floor of this cave is
ankle deep in 'em!"

They squelched on. At one point, they
disturbed a colony of bats who flew out of
the cave, their wings rustling like alarmed
umbrellas. Then suddenly, Captain

Thinscratch cried out as the candle-light gleamed on the brass locks of a treasure chest. The chest was standing on a rock in a hole in the cave wall.

Captain Thinscratch fell to his knees and ran his left hand over the chest. "'Tis mine!" he shouted. "Mine! I'm goin' to be the greatest pirate ever!"

With the point of his cutlass, Captain Thinscratch picked the locks on the chest and threw open the lid. "What in the name of Neptune...?" he gasped.

"Well, blow the man down!" murmured Benbow.

Instead of gold and jewels, the treasure chest was filled with shadows. Captain Thinscratch held the candle high as he scrabbled inside. "It must be 'ere!" he whispered frantically. "Maybe there's an 'idden compartment or – ah, what's this?"

He brought a neatly folded piece of parchment out of the chest. After setting the candle down on the edge of the rock, the captain unfolded the parchment and read out loud the words he found written on it.

If you're a pirate brave and bold,
Who came here hoping to find gold,
Prepare yourself to know the worst—
Tornado Truman got here first.

For a long time, there was silence in the cave, and then Crispin Chickweed said, "Oh well. Better luck next time, eh?"

And so Captain Thinscratch and the others turned back. They retraced their steps through the jungle, where the mambas hissed threateningly and the monkeys pelted them again, past the dodos, who pecked them cruelly, and on to the mangrove swamp, where the alligator chased them all the way to the longboat.

"All that for nothin'!" seethed the captain. "When we're back on board *The Purple Prawn*, I'm goin' to make you walk the plank."

"Um, I think you might 'ave a slight problem there, cap'n," said Dab.

"What problem?" demanded Captain Thinscratch.

"The ship's not there," said Dab.

It was true. The gap in the reef was empty and *The Purple Prawn* was nowhere to be seen. A small mound of provisions had been left on the beach together with a note which read:

Ahoy there, Captain Thinscratch, you swab!
We're fed-up with doing all the work while you get all the fame. When high tide lifts the ship off the reef, we're sailing away and leaving you and your friends here to rot.

We're going to join up with Tornado Truman — he's twice the pirate you are.
Best wishes,
The Crew.

Captain Thinscratch tore the note to
shreds, threw the shreds on to the sand and
jumped on them, swearing so fiercely that
Lucan the Toucan tucked his head under
one of his wings.

"I'll be revenged for this!" raved the
captain. "I'll keel-'aul every man-jack aboard
The Purple Prawn if it's the last thing I do!"

"Oh, give it up, skipper!" said Benbow.

"Aye!" said Mussels. "We're stuck on this island and that's that."

"Face facts, cap'n," said Dab. "Your days as a notorious pirate are over."

"My career, over?" shrieked Captain Thinscratch. "Never! Follow me back into the jungle, men. We're goin' to chop down some trees!"

"Are you taking up woodwork as a hobby?" asked Crispin Chickweed.

"No!" snapped Captain Thinscratch. "We're goin' to built a raft, and it's goin' to be the most rollickin' raft that ever sailed with a pirate as its captain!"

Captain Thinscratch walked up the beach towards the palm trees. Dab and Mussels went with him, but Benbow and Crispin Chickweed lingered on the beach a while.

"I bet you curse the day you ever joined up with Abel Thinscratch," said Benbow.

"No, not really," said Crispin Chickweed. "I know being a pirate means feeling seasick and being chased by alligators, pecked by dodos and pelted with rotten mangoes, but to tell you the truth, I haven't had so much fun for years!"